Squirrel's Fun Day

Lisa Moser

illustrated by Valeri Gorbachev

CANDLEWICK PRESS

For Madison, Michael, Kate, and Meg.
You fill the world with fun, fun, fun!
Love,
L. M.

For my son, Kostya, and my daughter, Sasha
V. G.

Text copyright © 2013 by Lisa Moser
Illustrations copyright © 2013 by Valeri Gorbachev

First edition 2013

Library of Congress Catalog Card Number 2012943653

ISBN 978-0-7636-5726-0

13 14 15 16 17 18 SCP 10 9 8 7 6 5 4 3 2 1

Printed in Humen, Dongguan, China

This book was typeset in Clarendon.
The illustrations were done in ink and watercolor.

Candlewick Press
99 Dover Street
Somerville, Massachusetts 02144

visit us at www.candlewick.com

Contents

Chapter 1

FOLLOW ME, ME, ME

Squirrel was busy, busy, busy.

He was going to have a very fun day.

"Got to go.

Got to go.

Got to go, go, go!"

Squirrel found Mouse at her tree stump. She was cleaning.

"Hello, hello, hello," said Squirrel. "Let's go have fun."

"Oh, no," said Mouse. "I can't have fun. I have too much work to do."

"Oh boy, oh boy, oh boy," said Squirrel. He swished his tail. "I am a great sweeper-upper. I will help you."

He dove into the stump. Mouse closed her eyes.

"Sweep, sweep, sweep!" yelled Squirrel.

Out flew the leaves for Mouse's nest.

"Sweep, sweep, sweep!" yelled Squirrel.

Out flew the fluff for Mouse's nest.

"Sweep, sweep, sweep!" yelled Squirrel.

Out flew the corn for Mouse's meals.

"Now can you have fun?" asked Squirrel.

Mouse looked at the mess. "I will have fun
if you stop sweeping," she said.

"Hooray!" said Squirrel. "Follow me, me, me!"

"Where do you go to have fun?" asked Mouse.

"Fun is everywhere," said Squirrel.

"You can have fun here." Squirrel crawled through a log.

"You can have fun here." Squirrel ran through the tall grass.

"You can have fun here." Squirrel jumped in a strawberry patch.

"What about here?" Mouse asked. She jumped on some leaves. She sank in the mud. "This is not fun," said Mouse. "I am stuck in the mud."

"Oh boy, oh boy, oh boy," said Squirrel. "I am a great getter-outer. I will help you."

Squirrel rolled a big strawberry to the mud hole. "I will throw, throw, throw this strawberry to you. You can stand on it. You can jump, jump, jump out of the mud."

Squirrel threw the strawberry.

SPLAT!

Strawberry dripped all over Mouse.

"I have another idea," said Squirrel. He held out a long piece of grass. "Hold on," said Squirrel. He pulled Mouse out.

"I am going to find more fun," said Squirrel.
"Do you want to come?"

"No, thank you," said Mouse. "I will stay here."

"Got to go.

Got to go.

Got to go, go, go!" said Squirrel.

He skipped to the pond.

Mouse licked strawberry off her whiskers.

Chapter 2
A BRIDGE FOR TURTLE

Squirrel found Turtle at the pond.

"Turtle? Is that you?" he called.

Turtle looked at his feet. Turtle looked at his shell. "Yup. It's me."

"Let's go have fun," said Squirrel.

"Do I have to get off my log?" asked Turtle.

"Yes," said Squirrel. "Follow me, me, me!" Squirrel ran around the pond.

Turtle took a step.

Squirrel ran back. "Run and follow me, me, me!"

Squirrel ran around the pond.

Turtle took a step.

Squirrel ran back. "Turtle!

You need to run, run, run."

"Yup," said Turtle.

"I am running."

Squirrel looked at Turtle. "Running *around*
the pond will take too long. I will help you go
across the pond. I will build a bridge."

Squirrel found a lot of rocks.

"Watch me build a bridge," said Squirrel.

He threw the rocks in the pond.

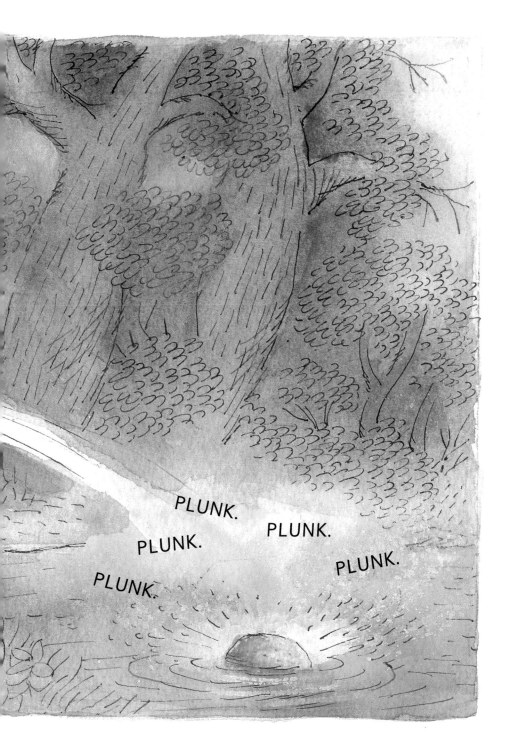

Turtle watched the rocks sink. "The rocks need to stick together to make a bridge," said Turtle.

Squirrel jumped up and down. "Oh boy, oh boy, oh boy! I know just what to do! I will stick them together with mud. I am a great mud maker."

Squirrel gave Turtle a big pile of dirt. "Hold this." Then Squirrel dumped water on the dirt.

"Dirt and water make mud," said Squirrel.

"Yup," said Turtle, dripping with mud.

"I have a plan, plan, plan," said Squirrel. "You build the bridge on this side of the pond. I will build the bridge on the other side. We will meet in the middle." Squirrel ran around the pond.

Squirrel dug and dug. Then he dumped water on the big pile of dirt.

"Oh, good," said a voice. "I came over to get more mud."

Squirrel looked closer. "Turtle? Is that you?"

Turtle looked at his feet. Turtle looked at his shell. "Yup. It's me."

"How did you get across the pond?" asked Squirrel. "I am not done with my bridge, bridge, bridge."

"I am a slow runner, but I am a fast swimmer," said Turtle.

"It is good that you went swimming," said Squirrel. "It cleaned you off. You were a muddy mess."

"Yup," said Turtle. "And now I need a nap."

He sat down in the sand. Squirrel patted his shell.

"Got to go.

Got to go.

Got to go, go, go!" said Squirrel.

He ran through the woods.

Turtle fell asleep.

Chapter 3
THINK BACKWARDS

Squirrel found Rabbit near his burrow.

"Hello, hello, hello," said Squirrel. "Let's go have fun." He jumped in a pile of pebbles. Pebbles rolled everywhere.

"Oh, no," said Rabbit. "I can't have fun. It's time for me to eat grass at the big oak tree."

"You eat grass at the same place every day?" asked Squirrel.

"I always do things the same way," said Rabbit.

"That's OK," said Squirrel. "We can have fun, fun, fun on the way."

"Follow me, me, me!" said Squirrel.

Rabbit picked up the pebbles. "I always leave a trail."

He dropped a pebble on the ground.

Squirrel ran to the meadow. He rolled in
the grass.

Rabbit took a step.

He dropped a pebble.

STEP.

PEBBLE.

STEP.

PEBBLE.

"Squirrel," said Rabbit. "I'm out of pebbles."

"Oh boy, oh boy, oh boy," said Squirrel. "I am a great pebble finder. I will help you." He ran down the trail. He came back with a pile of pebbles.

Squirrel ran to a waterfall. He splashed in the
water.

Rabbit took a step.

He dropped a pebble.

STEP.

PEBBLE.

STEP

PEBBLE.

"Squirrel," said Rabbit. "I'm out of pebbles."

Squirrel ran down the trail. He came back with a pile of pebbles.

"You are very fast at finding pebbles," said Rabbit.

"It is easy, easy, easy," said Squirrel. "There is a big line of pebbles behind us. I pick them up, up, up."

"Oh, dear," said Rabbit. "You picked up my trail! How will I get home?" His ears trembled. His whiskers twitched.

"Think backwards," said Squirrel.

Rabbit ran in circles. "Backwards think cannot I."

"Do not *talk* backwards," said Squirrel. "*Think* backwards. What did you see on the way?"

"I didn't see anything," said Rabbit. "I was leaving a trail."

"I saw lots of things," said Squirrel. He ran

up a tree. "I see some of them now!

I see the wet, wet, wet waterfall.

I see the soft, soft, soft meadow.

I see your burrow!"

He jumped down.

"Follow me, me, me!"

said Squirrel.

"We made it!" said Rabbit.

"Yes, yes, yes," said Squirrel. "Would you like to come with me and have more fun?"

"Oh, no," said Rabbit. "I always sit in the sun after I eat grass at the big oak tree."

"OK," said Squirrel. "Got to go.

Got to go.

Got to go,

go,

go!"

Squirrel danced over the hill.

Rabbit sat in the sun.

Chapter 4

CELEBRATE

Squirrel bounced in a patch of clover.

Squirrel jumped from tree to tree.

Squirrel ran through a field of flowers. "Oh boy, oh boy, oh boy," said Squirrel. "I will pick these flowers for my friends. We will celebrate our fun, fun, fun day."

Squirrel ran to Mouse's tree stump. "Mouse! I have flowers to celebrate our fun day."

But Mouse was not there.

Squirrel ran to Turtle's log. "Turtle!

I have flowers to celebrate our fun day."

But Turtle was not there.

Squirrel ran to Rabbit's burrow. "Rabbit!
I have flowers to celebrate our fun day."

But Rabbit was not there.

Squirrel walked home.

He thought about Mouse getting stuck.

He thought about covering Turtle with mud.

He thought about picking up Rabbit's trail.

Squirrel looked at his flowers. "Oh, oh, oh," cried Squirrel. "My friends did not have fun. They will never play with me again." Squirrel ran up to his nest and hid under the leaves.

Squirrel felt something bump his tail. He looked up. A little seed flew into his nest. *TINK.*

Squirrel looked down. He saw Mouse, Turtle, and Rabbit.

"You are throwing seeds at me because you are mad," said Squirrel. "I am sorry, sorry, sorry that you did not have fun today."

TINK.
TINK.
TINK.
TINK.
TINK.

"We are not mad," said Mouse.

"We are trying to wake you up," said Turtle.

"We want you to come down," said Rabbit.

Squirrel ran down the tree. "Oh boy, oh boy, oh boy," said Squirrel. "You are not mad?"

"Oh, no," said Mouse. "We had fun today! I stopped working and ate sweet strawberries."

"Yup. I got off my log and played in the mud," said Turtle.

"I did something different," said Rabbit. "I saw a pretty waterfall and a soft meadow on my way home. And I do not need a trail anymore. I know the way."

Squirrel jumped up and down.

"We have been making a surprise for you," said Mouse. "Follow us!"

They climbed to the top of the hill.

"We made a picnic," said Turtle.

"With strawberries," said Mouse.

"And starlight," said Rabbit.

Squirrel looked around. "And friends, best of all.

Oh, this is going to be fun, fun, fun!"